The
Golden Wasp*

A Magical World Awaits You
Read

THE
SECRETS
OF
DROON

#1 The Hidden Stairs and the Magic Carpet

#2 Journey to the Volcano Palace

#3 The Mysterious Island

#4 City in the Clouds

#5 The Great Ice Battle

#6 The Sleeping Giant of Goll

#7 Into the Land of the Lost

#8 The Golden Wasp

THE SECRETS OF DROON

The
Golden Wasp

by Tony Abbott
Illustrated by Tim Jessell

A
LITTLE APPLE
PAPERBACK

SCHOLASTIC INC.
New York Toronto London Auckland Sydney
Mexico City New Delhi Hong Kong

Book design by Dawn Adelman

ISBN 0-439-18298-0

12 11 10 9 8 7 6 5 4 3 2   0 1 2 3 4 5/0

Printed in the U.S.A.   40
First Scholastic printing, June 2000

For Jane and Lucy,
who make each day
a feast of joy and fun

Contents

One

The Moon in Droon

"Grrr! Ruff-ruff! Eeegg!"

Eric Hinkle and his best friends, Julie and Neal, jumped aside as a small dog raced across Eric's basement floor.

Except that it wasn't really a dog. It had four sharp ears, bright blue fur, a snubby pink nose, and long teeth. It growled and snarled.

And it came from another world.

A world called Droon.

"We've got to catch it, guys!" Eric cried. "We have a more serious problem, remember?"

"I'm not an *it*! I'm a moonfox!" the creature snapped. Then it bounced to the shelf above the dryer and began to chew it. *"Grrr-ruff! Ruff!"*

Julie swatted at it with a broom. "He's eating everything! We need to get him back to Droon!"

"And get my dad back *here*!" Eric cried.

Right. His dad. Mr. Hinkle.

He was the more serious problem.

Mr. Hinkle was in Droon, the strange, magical, and secret world below Eric's basement.

Droon was a world of wonder and adventure.

It was a world where an old wizard named Galen and a young princess named

Keeah battled a terrible sorcerer called Lord Sparr.

It was a world that only Eric, Julie, and Neal went to. Until now.

"I'll never go back!" the moonfox growled, scratching the window, then nibbling the frame.

Eric glanced around in a panic as his mind raced through the last twenty minutes.

He and Julie and Neal had just come back up the magical staircase that connected their world — the Upper World — to Droon. Then Julie noticed that she had left her charm bracelet behind.

And the one she wore was from Droon.

That was bad, very bad.

Galen had told them never to bring anything back from Droon. If they did, things would start going back and forth between the worlds.

And something did go. Eric's father.

First, he was here, then — *poof!* — he wasn't.

Unless they brought him back soon, other things might come here. Evil things.

Maybe even Lord Sparr himself!

Meanwhile, the charm on the Droon bracelet had come alive and was wrecking the basement.

Crunch — spah! The moonfox bit off a piece of Mr. Hinkle's tool bench, then spat it out.

"Oh, man!" Eric sighed. "What can we do?"

"Food!" yelled Neal suddenly.

"Will you *forget* food?" snapped Julie. "We have to trap this thing —"

"And food will do it!" Neal said. He dug into the seat of his favorite old armchair. He pulled out a handful of pretzels. "Good thing I'm a messy eater. Hey, moonfox, are you hungry?"

The fox screeched to a stop on a ceiling beam. "Am I *hungry*? Do I *look* hungry?"

Neal grinned. "Pretzels, here! Free pretzels!"

"Yes!" cried the fox. It jumped for the food.

In a flash, Eric grabbed a laundry basket and popped it over the fox. Julie piled some heavy cartons on top.

"I'll chew my way out!" growled the fox.

"Not before we get back!" Eric said, heading for the closet under the stairs. "Next stop, Droon. Time to find my father."

"And my bracelet," Julie added.

"And more food," said Neal as the three friends tumbled into the closet under the stairs.

Before Eric closed the door, he looked out at the basement one last time. His father's tool bench stood peacefully against the far wall. Sunlight fell through the window, flickering through the leaves of two apple trees outside his house.

Suddenly, Eric felt not just scared, but sad.

His father had taught him to climb those trees.

"He was teaching me guitar chords, too," Eric said. "I mean, what if Sparr finds him? What if somebody puts a curse on him? What if —"

"Come on, Eric," Julie whispered, pulling him into the closet. "We'll find him. We will."

Neal closed the door behind them. Julie switched off the light. The little room went dark.

Then — *whoosh!* — the floor beneath

them vanished and they were standing at the top of a long rainbow-colored staircase.

The steps shimmered in a pale light from below. It was moonlight from the land of Droon.

They stepped quickly down the stairs. They never knew where the staircase would take them, only that it would soon fade.

It always reappeared somewhere else in Droon when it was time to leave.

"I see a city," said Julie, peering down.

The moon had started to turn pale. Morning sun glinted off a giant stone palace.

Eric's heart raced when he realized where they were. "It's Jaffa City. Keeah will be here. She'll help us for sure!"

Jaffa was Droon's grand capital city. Princess Keeah lived there with her father, King Zello.

As they descended, the kids could see the palace courtyard bustling with people. Some were rushing here and there with blazing torches. Others were busily toting chests and bundles.

"Something's going on," Neal said as they left the staircase. "The whole city is out today."

Groups of six-legged, shaggy beasts called pilkas were stamping their feet near the city gates.

The sound of carriages squeaking on the cobblestones mixed with dozens of strange voices.

And one voice rang out above the others.

"Julie! Eric! Neal!"

"Keeah?" said Julie, scanning the courtyard.

"Here I am!" the princess called, waving from the crowd. Keeah wore a bright blue

tunic and leggings. A jeweled crown spar-
kled on her long golden hair. She ran to
greet the kids.

With her was her father, King Zello, a
fierce-looking man in a helmet with horns
sticking out of it. But he smiled when he
saw the kids.

"It's a wonderful day!" Keeah said. "All
the kings and queens of Droon are meeting
here. We are going to Zorfendorf for a cel-
ebration. . . ."

She stopped. "Eric, what's wrong?"

"It's not a wonderful day in my world,"
Eric said. "Something called a moonfox
is loose in my basement. Plus my dad's
lost . . . in Droon."

The king's smile faded. "We must tell
Galen immediately. His magic tower is
nearby —"

Before they could move, a figure clad all

in black jumped from the crowd. It ran so swiftly they couldn't make out who or what it was.

"Halt, creature!" Zello cried. "Who are you?"

But the figure sprang quickly at the king. It showered a sizzling jet of red sparks over him.

Then it lurched around and leaped at Keeah.

"Get away from us!" she cried. She shot a bolt of blue light from her fingertips. The creature dodged it and bounded away across the courtyard, scattering sparks over everyone it passed.

"What's he doing?" Neal asked.

"Let's find out!" said Eric.

Together they rushed after the dark shape. It bolted through the crowd toward the city wall.

"We trapped him!" Eric shouted.

The figure ran straight for the wall, then turned around to face them. Sort of.

"Yikes!" Neal blurted out.

Eric staggered back as the creature slid into the shadows and vanished in a puff of smoke.

Keeah and Julie rushed over to the boys.

"Who was it?" asked the princess.

"I don't know," Neal said. "But he had no —"

"F-f-face!" Eric stammered. "He had no *face!*"

Two

Under a Spell

Five minutes later, the kids were climbing to the top room of the wizard's tower.

They popped through a small door and into a large round room filled with clutter.

"Hail, friends from the Upper World!" Galen boomed happily. But when they told him everything that had happened, he brooded solemnly, stroking his beard. Finally, he spoke.

"Eric, your father must be found at

once. The balance between our worlds has been upset. Julie's bracelet stayed in Droon and another went to your world. As long as Mr. Hinkle remains here, someone from Droon can ascend the stairs."

Eric shuddered. "Someone? You mean Sparr?"

The wizard nodded. "Sparr has always wanted to spread his evil reign to the Upper World. With your father here, he has his chance."

Neal gulped. "I think I speak for everyone when I say — yikes!"

"Quite," said Galen. "As for this faceless creature, I must look him up!" He pulled a thick book from a shelf.

"The kings are nearly ready!" chirped a tiny voice. The kids looked up. Max, Galen's spider troll helper, swung through the window on a thread of silk.

Max's normally wild orange hair was parted in the middle and combed down flat. His clothes were new and neat. "Master Galen, may our friends come to Zorfendorf Castle, too?"

Galen shut his book. "I'm afraid our plans have changed. Children, the faceless creature you saw is called a *wraith*."

"What's a wraith?" asked Julie.

Max gasped softly. "A wraith is a victim of the Golden Wasp. Some pour soul stung by Sparr's evil insect."

The kids stared at one another.

On their last adventure, Lord Sparr had found an object of great magic called the Golden Wasp.

Its sting gave him the power to control people's minds. Now he was using it.

For evil, of course.

Eric had a sudden, frightening thought.

"What about my dad?" he asked. "What if Sparr finds him? What if the Wasp stings him?"

The wizard narrowed his eyes. "Sparr has made it more difficult to peer into his dark lands. I suggest we find Portentia. She is a truth teller, an oracle living in the Farne Woods. If anyone knows where your father is, it is she."

Der-der! A loud trumpet fanfare sounded from the courtyard below.

"The majesties are leaving!" Max chirped. "Oh, the Lumpies will eat everything!"

Keeah rushed to the window. "Father! Father!" she called out, waving her arms.

The kids had just spotted their old friends — Khan, the purple, pillow-shaped king of the Lumpies, and Batamogi, the furry ruler of the mole people — when a second trumpet sounded.

The pilkas thundered noisily toward the gate.

"Let's hurry and get down there," said Julie.

But by the time the children made it to the courtyard, the great royal caravan had gone.

The square stood deserted.

"My father was so excited," Keeah said. "I didn't even get a chance to say good-bye."

Eric sighed. "I know what that feels like."

"Come," said Galen. "Our journey lies another way, far from Zorfendorf Castle."

They left the courtyard through a small gate.

Beyond the walls lay a broad green meadow, and on its far side, a forest of tall trees.

Galen and Max led the band across the

meadow. They traveled as quickly as they could.

"Eric, I think your father is safe," Keeah said as they neared the huge woods. "I just feel it."

"I hope so," said Eric. Just yesterday, his father helped him with his math home-work. Then they played guitar together. Well, his father played, Eric mostly messed up. But it was fun.

Now he imagined waking up tomor-row without his dad at home. Tears rushed to his eyes.

"Hey, it'll be okay," said Neal, giving him a nudge. "We won't leave Droon with-out him."

Eric rubbed his eyes. "Um, Galen? What exactly happens if the Wasp stings you?"

The wizard turned to him. "You lose yourself, and your mind belongs to Sparr," he said. "No matter how good you are, you can be made to do bad things. After a while, you become a wraith."

Eric wanted to ask more questions, but Galen walked on in silence. The small troop continued in silence until they reached the foot of the great woods.

Everyone stopped. Julie and Neal looked at each other, then at the shadows of the forest.

"Well, what's stopping us?" Julie asked.

"Fear," said Neal. "Also fear. Plus . . . fear."

Keeah grinned. "So let's be afraid together."

The moment they stepped into the woods, the scent of pine was thick around them.

Galen and Max strode ahead. Cushions of brown needles rustled softly underfoot as they padded along. Tangled vines hung over the winding path. The kids rushed to keep up.

"Um, guys?" said Neal, ducking under a low branch. "Did I ever tell you how much I don't like dark and scary woods?"

Eric couldn't see Galen. He hurried his steps.

"Well, I don't," Neal went on. "They remind me of those creepy movies where you're walking along and suddenly —"

"Help!" Max yelped.

"It's Max! And he's in trouble," Julie cried, rushing ahead.

Two fierce, red-faced warriors had popped out of nowhere and were trying to pull Max into the bushes.

"Ninns!" Keeah yelled.

"Get away, you fiends!" Galen boomed, dashing down the path to Max. Six more large Ninns jumped from the shadows and grabbed him.

"Run!" Galen told the children. "Find Portentia! Her home is deep in the woods! Hurry!"

In a flash, a dozen more Ninns burst noisily from the bushes. "Get little ones!" they grunted.

"Let's move it!" Eric yelled.

The four children raced down the path as fast as their legs could carry them. Vines whipped their faces as they ran deeper into the woods.

Ten minutes later, out of breath, the kids stopped. Keeah raised her hand.

Everyone listened.

"No grunting, no stomping feet," said Neal. "Sounds like we lost them."

Suddenly — *kla-bamm*!

The sky exploded and the ground thundered.

The children fell to their knees. A sudden shower of hot pebbles rained over them.

Then a voice louder than the thunder boomed, "WHO D-D-DARES TO ENTER MY S-S-SACRED GR-GR-GROVE?"

Three

The Grove of Portentia

Before them stood a clearing. And at the back of the clearing sat a big gray boulder with a hole in the center.

"A talking rock?" Neal whispered. "Okay, I am out of here —"

"Don't be a scaredy-cat," said Julie.

"I see *you're* shaking," Neal retorted.

"S-S-SILENCE!" boomed the voice. As it did, another spray of pebbles spat out from the rock and fell over the grove.

"Say it, don't spray it," Julie mumbled.

"I AM P-P-PORTENTIA!" boomed the rock. "WHY HAVE YOU C-C-COME TO ME?"

Everyone looked at Eric. Quivering in fear, he stepped forward.

"We've come to ask you something," he said. "It's about —"

"SILENCE!" Portentia boomed. "First I speak, then you seek! From the dawn of time, my riddles rhyme! The secrets of Droon shall not be known soon! I speak only truth, and . . . I can . . . I shall . . . you must . . . oh, fiddlesticks!"

The stone began whispering and sputtering wildly. It sounded as if it was arguing with itself. Finally, a long sigh came from the hole.

"Oh, dear . . ."

"Portentia?" said Keeah. "Are you all right?"

"Oh, it's no use!" the stone said, spitting another tiny bit of gravel on the kids. "I try to be scary and spooky and all that. People expect an oracle to be loud and mysterious. But I don't really want to be. And *you* try rhyming all the time! Now, that's hard work!"

Julie started to laugh. Then Neal did.

Portentia began laughing, too. "Oh, I love the sound of laughter, don't you? Sounds are all I have, you know. I can't see a thing. But I sense quite a bit. And right now, I sense a boy with a problem. What can I do for you, dear?"

Eric stopped trembling. "Well, I need to know where my father is. Like me, he's from the Upper World and he's lost in Droon somewhere."

"Oh, dear, a lost father," Portentia said, sounding concerned. "And from the Upper World, too. That's not good. Is your father a king?"

Eric shook his head. "No, he's just a dad."

Portentia was silent for a moment, then said, "I see a man in plaid."

"That's the guy!" Neal shouted. "He always wears those work shirts with red and blue —"

"The man is hidden, in a city forbidden!"

Eric shivered. "Forbidden? You mean —"

"The fortress of Plud," said Portentia. "Sparr's home in the dark lands. Lots of wicked Ninns."

Eric remembered Plud from their first adventure in Droon. It was a horrible place. Dark and dreary.

"Your father is not hurt," Portentia said. "But you must find him soon."

"We will," said Eric firmly. He turned to go.

"Wait," said the oracle. "I see a bracelet. . . ."

"My bracelet!" said Julie. "That's what started it all."

"That's in Plud, too," Portentia replied. "And I also sense . . . a princess is with us?"

Keeah bowed. "I am the daughter of King Zello and Queen Relna. My name is —"

"Keeah!" Portentia cried. "Dear, dear, I knew your sweet mother. A great wizard of Droon."

The princess nodded. "She lives under a curse. I don't know where she is now."

Portentia sighed. "She has a long journey ahead, but — wait! I feel a riddle coming! A door to the past! A spell that is cast! The future of Droon is found in a tune! And, and . . . oh, well. That's all for today, I'm afraid. Most things I say don't make sense to me. Have I helped at all?"

Keeah nodded. "Yes. Thank you, Portentia."

The stone seemed to smile. "No, dear, thank *you*. I don't get many visitors. And now, for a big finish. GO! PORTENTIA HAS SPOKEN!"

Kla-bamm! Thunder clapped overhead, and one last rain of tiny pebbles splattered the kids.

They turned and made their way to the path.

"I like Portentia," Neal said as they neared the edge of the forest. "She talks like my grandma."

"I wonder what she meant," said Keeah. "'The future of Droon is found in a tune'?"

"Maybe we should all whistle," Neal said.

Eric was quiet. His father was in Plud. Sparr's fortress. Sparr's terrible, horrible home.

Keeah glanced at him, then hurried quickly along the path. "Come on," she said. "Plud is in the dark lands. We'll hurry —"

Suddenly, she stopped. She turned.

"What's wrong?" Julie asked, looking around.

"Lions?" Neal said. "Tigers? Bears? *Sparr?*"

Keeah stared into the thick trees. "The door to the past!" she said. "I . . . I . . . oh, my gosh!"

Without another word, Keeah raced deep into the forest. The three friends looked at one another.

"I guess we follow her," said Eric.

A chill wind blew swiftly through the trees.

"I guess we follow her *fast!*" cried Neal.

Four

Door to the Past

Eric, Julie, and Neal gasped when they saw it.

A cottage.

It was small and overgrown and nestled between two giant pine trees. A third tree twisted up out of the roof. A small room was built into its limbs, almost like a tree house.

"Where's Goldilocks?" Neal joked.

Julie chuckled. "If you mean Keeah, she

just went inside. Maybe we should follow her. Who knows what's in there?"

When they entered the house, Keeah was flitting around, touching everything in sight. It seemed as if she had found something that had been lost for a long time.

"What is this place?" asked Neal.

But Eric guessed. "Keeah grew up here."

"Yes!" Keeah exclaimed. "This was my home when I was small. My mother and father and I lived here for a while. I had nearly forgotten it."

Inside was a single room, neatly swept but deserted. It looked as if no one had been there for ages. A table sat in the middle, with three chairs around it. In one corner, a set of narrow stairs curved its way to the upper room in the tree.

"Oh, I had such fun here," said Keeah.

"Wow," said Neal. "Talk about a door

to the past. I guess Portentia was right about that."

"I hope she's right about my dad being safe," Eric said. "He probably won't be for long —"

"My room! My room!" Keeah said, spying the staircase in the corner and rushing to it.

She flew up the steps as if she had wings.

"I love to see her like this," Julie said.

Eric nodded. But he couldn't get his dad out of his mind. His father was in danger. And Sparr was up to something. Something big and bad.

The wind rustled noisily through the trees.

Eric went to the window. "Those Ninns are still out there. I know they are."

At home, at night, he would hear noises in the backyard. His father always took a look. It was never anything bad, just cats or something.

"We should go," he said. "Portentia told us —"

Suddenly — *plong! bling! thrum!* — strange music sounded in the upper room.

Then — *thomp! thomp!* — the ceiling quaked.

Then — "Help!"

"It's Keeah!" cried Neal, dashing up the stairs.

Keeah was backed against the bed in the tiny room. She was clutching a small, bow-shaped musical instrument. Her eyes were wide with fear. "I just touched this harp and . . . look!"

Thomp! Thomp! A metal candlestick marched heavily across the floor toward her.

Cloppety! Cloppety! A small stool had stretched its legs and was coming at her, too.

Finally, the little rug on the floor began to wrap itself tightly around Keeah's feet.

"It was my mother's harp," Keeah said. "I don't know how to play it! And I don't know what it's doing!"

Neal grabbed the rug, but it twisted away, yanking him off his feet. It jumped on him.

"Hey!" he protested. "I stand on rugs, they don't stand on me!"

The candlestick began stomping on Eric's feet.

"Ouch!" he howled. "Keeah, play something!"

"I'll try!" she said. She touched the strings.

The harp played what almost sounded like a tune. *Thrum! Bling! Pong! Bwang!*

The candlestick jerked to a halt. The stool stopped dancing. The rug fell limp on Neal.

"Whoa!" said Neal. "Good choice of tunes."

Everyone stared at the harp.

Keeah touched it again lightly. "It's called a bowharp. I had no idea it had powers."

"Maybe this is what you were supposed to find," Julie said. "'The future of Droon is found in a tune.' That's what Portentia said."

"Well, I hope dancing furniture isn't the future of Droon!" said Keeah.

"Maybe it'll help us when we get to Plud," said Neal.

Keeah smiled. "*If* I ever learn to play it."

"And *if* we ever get there," said Eric. "Can we please get going soon?"

The princess jumped to her feet. "You're right. We've stayed here long enough. Let's go."

She slung the harp over her shoulder, and they all piled out of the small cottage.

Keeah patted the door as she closed it. "I'll be back," she said. Then she turned. "Plud is in the dark lands. We have a lot of ground to cover."

"Plud," said Neal with a snort. "Take a left at No Good and head straight for Evil."

"Sounds inviting . . . not," said Julie.

Eric breathed deeply. "Let's get moving."

Without another word, the four friends headed down the path and out of the forest.

Two hours later, they started up a jagged range of steep hills. As they climbed, the ground turned darker and darker. Scattered trees stood like bony hands scratching at the sky.

The air grew smoky and foggy and foul.

"Let me guess, the dark lands?" asked Julie.

"I knew I smelled something bad," said Neal.

They crossed over a sharp ridge and stopped.

Below them stood a vast frozen lake. Next to it, a black castle. Lightning crackled overhead. Cold rain began to pelt down from the sky.

"Sparr's evil fortress," Keeah said. "Once you go in, it's hard to leave."

Eric shivered when he thought of Sparr's latest prisoner.

Five

Surprise Guests at Plud

The dark turrets and twisted towers of Lord Sparr's giant castle jutted to the sky. Troops of red-faced Ninn soldiers marched back and forth across the walls.

"Real cozy," said Julie. "Come on. Let's sneak in and out before Sparr even knows —"

Crack! A twig broke behind them.

"Ninns!" Neal gasped. In a blur of

speed, he shot up a tree. Julie jetted up right behind him.

Keeah and Eric hustled up, too. They all huddled quietly in the branches, waiting for Ninns.

But Ninns didn't come.

Hrrr! A shaggy pilka tramped over the hills toward them. On its back was a large man with a horned helmet. Behind him rode a purple, pillow-shaped creature. Next came a fox-eared king wearing a green crown.

"I can't believe it!" Keeah whispered. "It's my father. And Khan. And Batamogi! What in the world are they doing here?"

The entire procession of Droon's majesties trotted slowly up the hill.

"Maybe they're on their way to Zorfendorf?" said Julie.

Eric gaped at the procession. "But isn't Zorfendorf hundreds of miles away?"

"Yes!" Keeah said. "Father! Father! Up here!"

King Zello rode on.

"Hey, Khan!" yelled Neal. "How's it going?"

None of the majesties looked up.

"Why won't they answer?" Julie asked.

"They don't hear us," Eric said. "Or see us."

Suddenly, Batamogi burst into loud laughter.

"Shhh!" said Julie. "Plud is just over the hill!"

Then the kings broke into song.

*"In Zorfendorf's bright summer sun,
We'll have our feast of joy and fun!"*

"Bright summer sun?" Neal squinted at the rainy sky overhead. "Am I missing something?"

"No," said Keeah sharply. "They're imagining sunlight. They're under a spell. They've been tricked into coming here! They think that Plud . . . is Zorfendorf!"

Julia gasped. "That creepy no-face guy! Sparr sent him to shoot sparks at everyone in Jaffa City. He's the one who put the spell on them."

"If only I knew how to play this harp!" said Keeah.

Thomp! Thomp! A troop of Sparr's heavy-footed, red-faced Ninns marched after the procession, grunting to one another as they went.

The kings and queens kept singing, as if they didn't even see the Ninns.

"Why does Sparr want them?" Eric asked.

Keeah shook her head, then she began to tremble. "Oh, no! He wants to . . . to . . .

set the Wasp on them! To control their minds!"

The kids watched as the procession traveled over the hill to the fortress. Lightning flashed, and the rain came down even harder.

"We need to get down there," said Eric. "We've got a bunch of people to rescue now."

Making sure they stayed out of sight, the kids jogged quickly between the trees and down to the shore of the frozen lake.

Soon they were at Plud's rear gate. Julie crept over with Neal and pulled it open.

Inside, the thomping of Ninn feet mixed with the eerie echoes of the kings' song.

"They're going to the main court," Keeah whispered as they entered a dimly lit passage.

"Great," said Eric. "Sparr's living room."

They edged up two narrow flights of damp stairs, then along a dark hall to an open balcony.

They crouched behind the balcony railing. Below them stood a large, empty room. It was dark and cold and dreary. The walls were black.

"Okay, now what?" said Julie peering down.

"A spell spell," said Keeah, giving the kids a little smile. "I've always wanted to try one. It allows you to see what a spell is like but not be under it. Hold my hands." They did.

Then Keeah whispered, *"Empa — tempa — roo!"*

A cool, tingling sensation passed from Keeah to the others. A moment later —

Der-der! A trumpet blast announced

the guests, and a brilliant flash of light illuminated the great hall.

"Holy crow!" Eric gasped softly.

A fire blazed suddenly in the hearth. Wall torches and candles shed golden light everywhere, making the giant room bright and cheery.

"Sparr is making the place beautiful!" said Julie.

Each high wall was hung with a rich tapestry showing one of the great castles of Droon.

In between, the stones bloomed with festive holly boughs, their red berries dotting the spiky leaves like rubies.

The center of the room was filled by a long wooden table. On it were platters heaped with food and goblets brimming with drinks.

"This is exactly what Zorfendorf looks like," Keeah said. "Down to the last detail.

This must be what my father and the others are seeing."

"And here they come!" Neal announced.

Garlands of red and gold ribbons fluttered over the doors, and the majesties entered. King Zello strode in at the head of the line. Beside him walked a tall, slender, green-furred creature.

"That's Ortha, queen of the Bangledorn monkeys," Keeah whispered. "And following her is Mashta, flying empress of the sand children."

Soon the leaders of every clan and tribe in Droon were assembled in the great room.

Following them was a small army of young serving people. They carried even more platters overflowing with fruits and meats.

"I wonder if that food's real," Neal whispered.

"Ah, Zorfendorf Castle!" boomed King Zello, taking his seat near the head of the table. "My home away from home! And where is our splendid young host, Prince Zorfendorf?"

All the guests raised their silver goblets, clanked them together, and called for their host.

"Prince Zorfendorf!" the crowd cheered.

The trumpets sounded again. Everyone turned to the door. The hall rang out with louder cheers as a handsome young man entered.

"It's him!" Keeah gasped, trembling.

"How can you tell?" said Julie.

"I can tell," Neal sneered. "It's yucko himself. Lord Sparr!"

Six

The Sting of the Wasp

It *was* Sparr. But he didn't look like himself.

He appeared young and handsome. He was dressed in a bright green tunic, a red sash, and black boots. Even the weird fins that normally grew behind his ears were missing.

He grinned as he entered the hall.

"He looks like a TV star!" Julie whispered.

"Yeah," said Eric. "The star of *The Evil Show*!"

Sparr greeted his guests happily. "Kings and queens of Droon! You have come to welcome Droon's glorious summer!"

Cheers rose from the crowd. "Here! Here!"

"But first, let us welcome someone else," the sorcerer went on. "I want you to put your hands together for . . . Lord Sparr!"

The crowd went silent. Then Khan laughed. "Surely you're joking! Welcome that evil man?"

Sparr said nothing.

King Zello put down his goblet. "We will never welcome Sparr! Besides, the fiend is in Plud!"

The sorcerer grinned. "And so, my dear king, are you!" He waved his hands over the room.

Before anyone could move —

Blam! Blam! The doors slammed shut.

Sparr's own handsome face fell away to reveal his usual ugly features. His ear fins flared from purple to rich, deep red.

The bright candles and torch flames flashed, then went out. The colorful tapestries ripped into tattered black cloth, drooping on the walls.

"What is happening?" Queen Ortha cried out.

Sparr laughed as the bright green holly shriveled into weeds. The platters vanished, and in their place appeared a gold cage covered by a black cloth.

Finally, the troop of young serving people spun around and became an army of Ninn guards.

"The spell is broken," Keeah said, letting go of everyone's hands. "Everyone sees the truth."

"Free us this instant!" demanded King Zello. He reached for his sword.

Two Ninns seized the king tightly.

"Him go to dungeon? With wizard and troll and man in strange clothes?" one Ninn asked.

"Strange clothes?" Eric whispered. "My dad!"

"No, no," the sorcerer replied, smiling coldly. "I have a gift for King Zello! Wraith, come here!"

As if it took shape from the shadows themselves, the faceless wraith suddenly appeared.

"Oooh, I don't like that guy," Julie whispered.

The wraith pulled the cloth from the cage on the table. Inside was a large gold insect, humming loudly. Its sleek wings flicked rapidly on the cage walls.

"The Golden Wasp!" Keeah hissed.

"We have to get down there," Julie said.

"Not yet," the princess replied. "We're outnumbered. We need to free these prisoners first. We need all the help we can get."

"Evil creature!" King Zello shouted. "You shall not harm us!" But before he could free himself, Sparr opened the cage.

"Wasp . . . strike!" Sparr commanded.

The insect fluttered its wings and shot over to the king. Zello struggled to escape, but the Wasp struck like lightning. Its tail curled and flicked the king sharply on the forehead.

Keeah winced as her father staggered back.

"What about the harp?" asked Eric. "Can't we use its magic now?"

"I don't know what powers it has," Keeah said. "What if I make things worse?"

Suddenly, King Zello straightened up.

He broke into a big smile. "Lord Sparr!" he boomed. "How may I serve my wonderful new master?"

"This is outrageous!" Batamogi cried. He and Khan ran at Sparr. The Wasp stung them on the way. Ortha, queen of the monkeys, bounded for the door. She was stung before she reached it.

Again and again, the Wasp attacked, until all the royalty of Droon had been stung.

Together, they stared at Lord Sparr.

Together, they bowed before him.

Together, they spoke in one voice.

"What would make you happy, Lord Sparr?"

The sorcerer cast his fiery eyes over the crowd. "In a room far below, I have some *gifts* for you. You will take them back to your own countries."

"Gifts, huh?" whispered Neal. "Something tells me they won't be fun."

"But there is more, my slaves!" Sparr went on. "In my dungeon down below is a man from the Upper World. As long as he is here, I can ascend the stairs. With your help, I shall conquer Droon. With *his* help, I shall conquer the Upper World! Yes, my slaves! I . . . shall take his place!"

Eric nearly choked. "What? What? That . . . that can't happen! Take . . . his . . . *place?*"

The majesties of Droon cheered over and over.

"Eric . . ." Keeah's hand was on his shoulder. Her eyes were moist, but she managed a smile. "It won't happen, I promise. Let's go find him. And Max. And Galen."

"And my bracelet," said Julie. "It's up to us to get things back to normal."

"Yeah," said Neal. "Before Sparr starts moving his stuff into your basement!"

But as Keeah pulled them along, Eric feared that nothing would ever be normal again.

Quietly, they hurried down the stairs.

To the dungeon.

Seven

The Locked Room

They entered a dark tunnel under the fortress.

With each step, Eric felt himself drawing closer to his father. He was here. Eric could feel it.

"I say we find the prisoners first," said Keeah. "Then the bracelet. I don't want us to split up."

Julie nodded. "Good idea."

"We should follow our noses," said Neal. "The dungeon's gotta smell the worst."

Eric winced. Neal was probably right. He wondered how his father was handling being in Droon. He sure wasn't seeing the best part of it.

As they went deeper into the dark passage, they heard a faint droning sound in the distance.

Nnnn. Nnnn. It sounded like a motor.

"Weird place," Eric said. "But I definitely think we're getting close."

"Close? We're here!" Neal said. He pointed to a door with a sign over it.

The sign read DUNGEON.

Julie laughed. "Nice of Sparr to label things."

"He probably had to, so the Ninns wouldn't get lost," Keeah said with a smile.

Together, they pulled open the heavy door.

They stepped into a room lit by the dim glow of a single wall torch. Eric spied three figures in chains. None of them was moving.

"Please let one of them be my dad," he said softly. "And please let him be okay."

They edged closer.

"It's called plaid," one voice said. "It comes in lots of colors. You can even get plaid pants!"

"Is that so?" said another excitedly. "I've seen the pattern before, but I can't remember where!"

"I wonder if I can weave plaid with my spider silk," chirped the third. "It looks quite soft."

Eric stepped into the light. "Um . . . hello? Dad?"

"Eric!" cried his father, his face beaming. "Holy crow! Why didn't you ever tell

me about this Droon place? And right under our house!"

"Ah," said Galen cheerfully. "Our rescuers have arrived. I told you, Sir Hinkle. They would never fail us."

Eric blinked at his father. "*Sir* Hinkle?"

Max rattled his eight chains. "Not exactly the feast of joy and fun we were all expecting!"

"Now, Keeah," said Galen. "A number-two blue bolt should release us. I would have done it myself, only the angle wasn't right. I didn't want to zap us all to Agrah-Voor!"

Keeah raised her hands and narrowed her eyes. "Stand back!" she said. A sudden bolt of blue light shot neatly from her fingertips.

Kzzz-zamm! The chains crumbled into a dusty heap on the floor. The prisoners were free.

Eric hugged his father. It felt strange to do that in front of his friends, but it felt good, too. Things were getting back to normal. Sort of.

Neal told Galen what was happening. "Sparr's Wasp stung all the majesties. Now he's sending them back to conquer their countries for him."

"And I need to find my bracelet right away," said Julie. "Sparr will probably use it to keep the door open so he can get to the Upper World."

Neal nodded. "There isn't a room marked BRACELET around here, is there?"

Mr. Hinkle blinked. "Almost! I think we passed a sign that said LOCKED ROOM. Galen, do you think maybe Sparr is keeping the bracelet there? Galen?"

But the wizard's eyes were fixed on Keeah's harp. "Forgive me," he said, a smile creeping over his lips. "I had thought that old harp was lost forever. It makes me happy to see it. Droon's ancient past lives again. It gives me much hope."

Keeah made a face. "Except that I can't play."

Galen nodded. "You will, Princess, when the time is right. Now, come. We are wasting time."

They left the dungeon.

Five minutes later they stood before a tall iron door set into the stone. The door had a huge padlock on it and a sign that read LOCKED ROOM.

Nnnn. The droning was loud behind the door.

"What's Sparr got cooking in there?" Neal wondered out loud.

Galen turned to Keeah. "Pluck the third string of the harp."

The princess did. *Brum!*

Ploink! The lock popped off, and the door sprung open.

"It does work!" Keeah said, beaming.

The room inside seemed to glow. The walls narrowed to a point at the ceiling.

And the droning was even louder.

Julie gasped. "It's here!"

The bracelet — her silver charm bracelet — was sitting alone on a tall stand in the center of the room. She darted over to it.

"It's strange that no one is guarding it," said Keeah.

Eric looked around. Up and down the walls were thousands of little holes, all exactly the same size. And the humming was coming from all around them. "I'm not so sure. . . ."

Julie took the bracelet from the stand and slipped it on. "Yes! It's mine! Things will be normal again, I know they will."

Something moved in one of the holes. The humming grew louder.

"What was that?" said Mr. Hinkle.

Eric stepped over to him. "I saw it, too."

Something else moved. Galen edged closer.

Zzzt! A tiny golden object shot out of a hole and buzzed around his head. He swatted at it. It buzzed back into its hole.

The humming grew still louder.

Then Galen knew. They all knew. He staggered backward. "Oh, dear, no!" he cried. "We're in . . . we're in . . . a nest!"

The walls were suddenly alive. The holes swarmed with thousands of tiny wasps.

"These must be the children of the Golden Wasp," Galen said, pulling the kids toward the door. "Sparr set them to guard Julie's bracelet."

Eric's eyes gaped. "Sparr said he was giving the kings gifts to help them conquer their countries. These wasps . . . are the gifts!"

Galen's face flashed with fear and anger. "We must stop him. Quickly, children, find the kings. Take them to safety!"

"But Sparr has them under his control!" Julie said. "They'll do only what *he* says!"

The wizard turned to Keeah. "Princess, you are your mother's daughter. I had not thought it possible, but you have found her lost harp. You must learn its power before you are truly ready. But it may be our only hope against Sparr."

Keeah looked at her mother's old harp.

Galen took her by the shoulders. "Go into the depths of your mind and bring up the memory of what she played to you.

Only love can conquer Sparr's evil. Only you can defeat him today. Go! Save your father. Save Droon!"

Keeah looked into the wizard's eyes. All of a sudden, they seemed very old.

"But what about you¿" she asked.

"I must stay here. I have business to do. Go!"

Mr. Hinkle and Max rushed the kids out of the room. Galen slammed the door behind them.

Lightning crackled from inside the room.

The humming grew louder.

Eight

Sparr's Wicked, Wicked Plan

The rain was even colder when they snuck into the outer courtyard. They hid behind a row of barrels and peered over.

Lord Sparr was on a high wall, looking down.

Below him, the majesties of Droon stood smiling blankly up at him.

"Ninns!" the sorcerer boomed. "Let us begin!"

A long line of his warriors tramped into the courtyard. Each one held an empty golden cage.

"Go, my soldiers!" Sparr cried. "Fill your cages with the children of the Wasp! Then you shall bring my gifts to every land in Droon!"

Saluting, the Ninns trudged into the fortress.

"So it's true," whispered Keeah. "Sparr is sending those wasps back with the kings. Then every good soul in Droon will belong to Sparr!"

Mr. Hinkle scanned the courtyard. "I don't know much about Droon, but this looks bad."

"It *is* bad, Sir Hinkle," said Max. "*Very* bad."

Eric wasn't sure they could do anything to stop Sparr. But he knew they had to try.

He turned to Keeah. "Galen said you need to remember the songs your mother played."

Keeah shook her head. "It seems so long ago. I don't remember anything."

"Yeah, my dad teaches me songs, too," Eric replied. "Sometimes I forget. Then I just start playing. It helps me remember."

Sparr mumbled a word, and his wraith slithered from a dark corner and stood next to him.

"Well, King Zello," the sorcerer called down, "how do you like serving me?"

"I love it!" the king boomed up happily.

"Good!" Sparr replied. "For soon you'll end up like my wraith here. A mere shadow!"

Keeah growled with anger, then closed her eyes. "Mother, help me to remember."

A moment later, a red-faced Ninn charged out of the fortress. "F-F-F."

Sparr snarled at him. "Well? What is it?"

"F-FIRE!" the Ninn cried. "Nest on fire!"

Thick smoke poured up suddenly from below.

Sparr flew down from the wall. "No! My glorious plan must not fail! Ninns, follow me to the nest. Wraith — summon your brothers!"

Eric gulped. "That thing's got . . . *brothers?*"

Sparr roared into the fortress. His red-faced guards chugged noisily after him as the wraith vanished back into the shadows.

"Now's your chance, Keeah," said Julie.

The princess looked over at her father. Then she looked at her friends and nodded firmly.

Lifting the harp, she began to play.

Bling! Thrum! Bimm! Keeah's fingers

moved magically over the strings as if she suddenly remembered an old song. She played more and more as the sound swirled around the courtyard.

Blim! Ping! Bong! Thoom!

The majesties of Droon began to stir. They blinked once. Then again. They looked around. Then they began to mumble to one another.

"The kings are themselves again," Max said.

"The spell is broken!" Julie exclaimed. "Keeah, you did it!"

King Zello turned as if awakened from a deep sleep. He gasped to see his daughter there. And he gasped when he saw the high black walls of the fortress. "Keeah . . . where are we?"

The princess rushed to her father and hugged him. "We're in Plud, Father. But we must all leave now. Quickly, this way! To the gate!"

Mr. Hinkle dashed over to help. "Hi, I'm Eric's dad. I think we'd better move out fast. That Sparr guy is mad we're messing up his plans."

King Zello slapped Eric's father on the shoulder. "Good to have your help, Sir Hinkle! Majesties of Droon, let's go!"

Neal nudged Eric. "Look at that. King Zello and Sir Hinkle. Two cool dads."

"Yeah," said Eric proudly. "Very cool!"

"Our problems aren't over yet," said Keeah.

Zzzt! The Golden Wasp shot out from the fortress. It looked mad. It sounded mad.

"Uh-oh, I think it's mad!" Eric yelled.

Neal threw a stone at it. The Wasp buzzed in a circle, then stopped. It looked at Neal. Then it flicked its wings rapidly. Then it shot after him.

"It's mad, all right," said Neal. "At me!"

Neal took off as the Wasp chased him into the burning fortress.

The kids stared at one another.

"After him!" they yelled.

Nine

Fire and Ice

"Help! Help! *Helllllp!*"

Neal's cries for help echoed in the dark halls.

Eric, Keeah, and Julie rushed after him until they reached the main court.

The Wasp had Neal backed into a corner.

"You're trapped!" said Eric, looking around.

"You think?" Neal shouted. "Do something!"

The Wasp hovered over Neal. Its tail twitched near his face. The long stinger waved back and forth in front of his nose. It came closer, closer.

Keeah ran over. Blue sparks shot off the tips of her fingers. "Neal — duck!"

"Looks like a big insect to me!" Neal said.

"Get down!" she shouted. He did.

Kla-bamm! Keeah's shot of blue light blasted the Wasp. It was thrown into the wall behind Neal.

ZZZZT! The Wasp was up before they left the room. The kids raced through dark halls, down stairs, and along dim passages.

They stumbled and ran and ran and stumbled until they could run no more.

Suddenly, it wasn't dark anymore. The walls of the passage glowed yellow and red.

"The nest!" Julie gasped, peering ahead.

The wild humming of the other wasps was nearly drowned out by the roar of the fire. Red, yellow, and blue flames licked the ceiling of the room Galen had set on fire.

Zzzzt! The Golden Wasp saw the burning nest, gave out a shriek, and shot in over the kids.

Inside the nest, Galen stood facing Sparr and his troop of Ninns. The wizard narrowed his eyes. "Your plan is finished, evil one! Give up!"

"Too late," the sorcerer snarled. "My plan has already begun. The strangers shall not leave Droon. Even now the stairs appear in my dark lands. I will ascend them. You cannot stop me."

Keeah ran in and stood next to Galen. "Oh, I think you'll be surprised —"

Sparr let out a long hissing noise. "Ah,

the princess. Good. Now you can perish together!"

Kla-bamm! He hurled a red lightning bolt at them. Galen and Keeah twirled out of the way.

At the sound of the blast, the Ninns bolted past the kids, scurrying for cover.

"Children, go!" Galen called out. "We will meet you outside!"

"But, Keeah —" Julie said.

"I'll be all right," the princess said with a smile. She tapped her harp. "Now, go!"

Kla-bamm! Sparr leveled another blast. Keeah blocked it with one of her own. The room lit up.

"We better get out of here!" Neal yelped.

The three friends charged through the passage and up the stairs. They tumbled out to the main courtyard where Mr. Hinkle and Max were waiting for them.

"The stairs are across the lake!" Max said.

Eric turned around. All of Plud was on fire.

Black smoke rose up, then fell over the lake.

"It's like the end of the world," Neal said. "And I'm not ready!"

"We need to go now!" Max said, running for the gate.

Eric shook his head. "I have this weird feeling we've forgotten something."

"I have my bracelet," said Julie.

"And you have me!" said Mr. Hinkle.

"Come, Eric," Max said, pulling the children gently out the gate. "Galen and Keeah will be fine. Together they are more powerful than Sparr. Keeah proved that today. Now, come."

The flames roared higher and higher as they all ran to the shore. King Zello and the others were already halfway across the ice. The magic staircase stood glistening on the far side.

The kids started across the lake. They were nearing halfway when Eric stopped. He turned around.

A wall of black smoke was rolling across the ice toward them. Eric stared at it. He listened.

"Son, what is it?" his father asked.

"I just remembered what we forgot," said Eric.

A sound was coming from behind the smoke.

Sloosh . . . sloosh . . .

It was the sound of metal on ice.

Suddenly, there it was. The wraith. It burst out from the smoke and skated toward them.

Sloosh . . . sloosh . . .

It was joined by another. Then another.

And another. An army was skating toward them.

"Mr. No-face . . . and his brothers," said Julie.

"I think we better move it," said Neal.

Eric nodded. "I think . . . you're right!"

Ten

The Harp and the Wasp

The kids tore across the ice, slipping and sliding toward the glittering staircase.

"We're never going to make it," Max chittered. "The wraiths are too fast!"

Suddenly — *ka-whoom!*

Plud's highest tower exploded into bits.

"Oh, my gosh!" Julie cried. "Keeah! Galen!"

Then — *whoosh!* *whoosh!* — Galen flew out of the flaming fortress. Behind him, Keeah was flying, too. She held her harp in front of her. It was pulling her swiftly through the air.

"Awesome!" Eric exclaimed. "They made it!"

"So did *they*!" Neal said, pointing to two dark streaks zooming across the sky.

The black flaps of Sparr's long cloak glistened like crow wings as he swooped after Keeah. The Golden Wasp followed close behind.

"Come, wraiths! Come, Ninns!" Sparr called out. "We will all ascend the stairs!"

Kla-bamm! His angry blast struck the sky near the wizards. Keeah was thrown down through the air. She tumbled to the lake near the kings.

Her father scooped her up instantly, but the harp struck the ice, bounced, and slid away from her. "Don't let Sparr get it!" Keeah cried out.

Eric dashed over and snatched up the harp. It seemed to hum in his hands. He knew instantly: *There is power in this harp.*

"Come, wraiths!" Sparr howled. "Onward, Ninns! Don't let them get to the stairs!"

Sloosh! Sloosh! The wraiths skated closer. The Ninns charged across the ice.

"We need a spell to stop them," said Julie.

"Keeah and Galen have their hands full with Sparr," Neal said, looking around wildly.

Eric stared at the harp in his hands. He turned to his father and held it out to him. "Play this, Dad."

"What?" his father said, shaking his head. "This is magic. I can't do magic. I'm just a dad."

"You taught me chords," said Eric. "You

taught me lots of stuff. You have to play it! Or Sparr will get into our house. Our world!"

Sloosh! The wraiths were racing over the ice.

Mr. Hinkle looked at Eric, then took the harp. "Here goes nothing." He touched the strings.

Plong! Ploink! Bloing! Plinkkkk!

"I thought you could play!" Neal groaned, slapping his hands over his ears. "That hurts!"

Suddenly, *kkkk*!

A crack appeared in the ice. It widened. The frozen lake split into dozens of pieces.

"Whoa, Mr. H.," said Julie. "You *can* play!"

The wraiths slid to a stop at the edge of the crack. They could go no farther.

The Ninns weren't so lucky.

"Argh! Ooof!" *Splash!*

The clumsy, red-faced warriors crashed into one another. Then they plopped into the icy water.

"Dad, you did it!" Eric shouted. "You did it!"

"To the stairs! Quick!" Keeah yelled, running over to them. They all skittered across the ice and bolted up the bank to the waiting stairs.

Kla-bamm! Galen fired a bolt of light at Sparr, stunning him, then joined the kids on the stairs. Together they ran to the room at the top.

Sparr leaped desperately after them, howling, "The Upper World is mine. Strike, Wasp, strike!"

"Here, Keeah," said Mr. Hinkle, handing her the harp. "It's time to do your stuff."

The Golden Wasp shot toward Keeah.

"Princess, prepare to become mine!" Sparr cried, climbing up after them. "Wasp — strike!"

Keeah stood firmly on the stairs, the cold wind blowing around her. She touched the strings.

Eric knew at once. The melody she played came from somewhere deep in her memory.

"Wasp — strike her!" Sparr cried again.

The Wasp did strike. It struck quickly.

But not at Keeah.

For an instant, it hovered over her, entranced by the melody she was playing. Then it lowered its tail and shot over to Sparr.

"Away! Away!" the sorcerer shouted.

But the Wasp would not obey him. It swept in and stung him — *ZZZZZZT!*

The sorcerer gasped, clutching his fore-head. "No! No! The Upper World belongs to me. I must — must — *akkkgh!*"

Sparr howled angrily as he plummeted — half flying, half falling — to the frozen lake below.

Eric trembled all over, staring at the sorcerer.

Sparr lay thrashing on the ice, yowling and roaring as his Ninns slid across the lake to him.

Behind him, the black fortress of Plud was red with flame.

"It is over, for now," Galen said. "Come. . . ."

Eric stared at the ice below. Even from that far away it seemed as if Sparr's fiery eyes were glaring at him. Piercing right to his heart.

It is not over.

That's what those eyes told him.

Julie tugged Eric to the top of the stairs. "The moonfox broke out. He's making another mess."

Eric ran through the closet into the basement.

Sunlight shone in as it had when they left.

"Holy cow!" Mr. Hinkle cried. "What a mess!"

The moonfox had eaten its way out of the laundry basket. Now it was tearing the stuffing out of the old chair.

"Hey, that's where I sit!" Neal yelled.

"I'll take care of him," Galen said, lurching into the basement with Keeah. He stared at the creature and thrust out his hands.

"Zof — kof — peechu — meechu — mack!"

The moonfox turned to Galen with his mouth full of stuffing. "Wait, no —"

Bloink! He vanished in a puff of green air. In his place, a gold charm bracelet clattered to the basement floor.

Max scampered over, snatched the Droonian bracelet, and dropped it into a pouch on his belt.

He beamed. "And that's that!"

"Hooray!" Julie cried. "It's over!"

Everyone breathed a sigh of relief.

Mr. Hinkle just stood staring at the whole thing. "Boy, Eric, wait till I tell your mother."

Galen smiled. "That reminds me. Sir Hinkle?"

"Yes, Galen?"

"Somban — romban — toop!"

Eric's father gave a sudden wiggle, then a giggle, then he stared ahead. Then his eyes slammed shut. And he started humming.

"Your father is forgetting everything that happened to him," Galen said to Eric. "Droon must remain a secret known only to the chosen ones."

"Chosen ones?" said Neal. "I like that."

Eric sighed. He knew Galen was right.

"Sorry, Dad," he said softly. "It was fun."

Mr. Hinkle coughed, then sneezed, then his eyes popped open. "Um . . . what just happened? I mean . . . where . . . um . . . what . . . Oh, never mind! Just clean up this mess, will you?"

"Yes, sir!" said Julie.

Mr. Hinkle turned. "For some reason, I like when you call me *sir*." Then he tramped upstairs, scratching his head.

"Galen, we'd better leave now," Keeah said to the wizard. She headed to the closet, then turned and smiled at Eric. "Once again, you have —"

Keeah glanced behind him. Her eyes widened suddenly. She pointed out the basement window at the trees outside. She began to tremble.

"What's wrong?" Julie asked.

"Those trees —" she said.

"Apple trees," Eric said. "My dad taught me how to climb on those trees."

Keeah stared at the sun winking through the bright green leaves of the twin trees.

"I've . . . been here . . . before," she said.

Eric felt as if lightning had struck him. "What? What? But . . . how is that *possible*?"

"I don't know," Keeah said. "I . . ."

"Hurry!" Max called from the closet. "The stairs are fading. We must not stay!"

Keeah turned to the wizard. "Galen,

could this be true. Could I have been here before?"

He pulled Keeah gently to the stairs. "All things are possible. But this is a mystery for another day. Come, Princess, we must leave here!"

He rushed into the closet with Keeah and Max.

Eric ran in and looked down as the three of them sped down the stairs and into the pink sky.

Keeah kept looking back until she disappeared into the clouds below.

Julie and Neal stood next to Eric, holding the door open until the stairs faded completely.

No one spoke for a long time. Finally, Eric flicked on the light in the closet.

Whoosh! The floor appeared. Droon vanished.

Eric turned to his friends. "What Keeah said . . . It's impossible, right?"

Neal restuffed the chair and slumped down into it. "Been here before? I mean . . . when?"

Julie bit her lip and shook her head. "Talk about secrets? You guys, that's gotta be Droon's biggest one yet!"

Eric nodded. "Something tells me we're just beginning to discover the real secrets of Droon."

"And you know what that means?" said Neal. "Lots more adventures!"

Eric smiled. Adventures. That sounded good.

He turned to his friends. Then he glanced out the basement window to the yard outside.

"Hey, guys, who feels like climbing a tree?"

"I do!" said Neal, springing up from the chair.

"Me, too!" said Julie, jumping ahead of him.

Eric joined them on the stairs as they raced out to the backyard to play.

ABOUT THE AUTHOR

Tony Abbott is the author of more than three dozen funny novels for young readers, including the popular *Danger Guys* books and *The Weird Zone* series. Since childhood he has been drawn to stories that challenge the imagination, and like Eric, Julie, and Neal, he often dreamed of finding doors that open to other worlds. Now that he is older — though not quite as old as Galen Longbeard — he believes he may have found some of those doors. They are called books. Tony Abbott was born in Ohio and now lives with his wife and two daughters in Connecticut.